MW00884588

Monster Hunter

Written and Illustrated by

JUSTIN LAROCCA HANSEN

Sky Pony Press
New York

Billy Banks was a monster hunter. It was a good thing too, because Billy's house was infested with monsters. They were in the closets and hallways, under the beds and carpets. It was Billy's job to get rid of them. Unfortunately, getting rid of monsters could get pretty messy.

Like on Monday when a monster left his room covered in slime. His mother was not pleased. Billy told her, "It wasn't me, Mom! It was a monster!" But for some reason the monsters only came out when he was by himself. Like on Sunday night when Billy had to battle the . . .

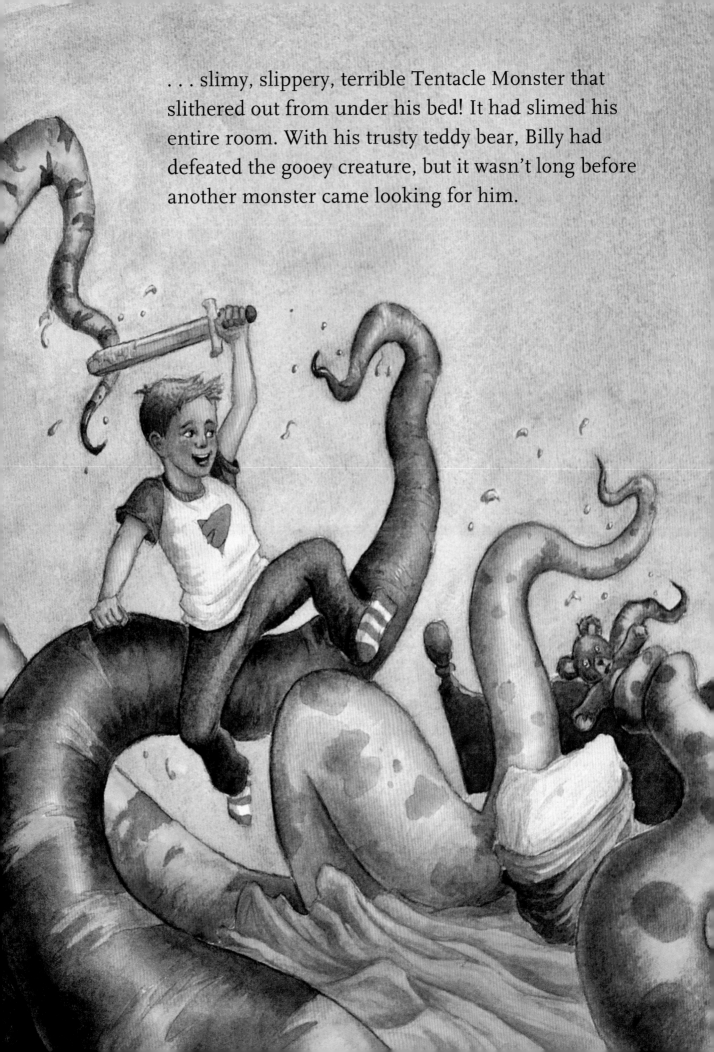

. . . slimy, slippery, terrible Tentacle Monster that slithered out from under his bed! It had slimed his entire room. With his trusty teddy bear, Billy had defeated the gooey creature, but it wasn't long before another monster came looking for him.

On Tuesday, Billy's mother found huge puddles of water on the bathroom floor and made him clean them up. Once again Billy said, "It wasn't me, Mom! It was a monster!"

This time it had been a troublesome
Tuna Monster, trying to climb out of the
toilet. After some plunging, Billy was able
to flush the floundering, flailing fish back
into the deep, dark depths of the sewer.

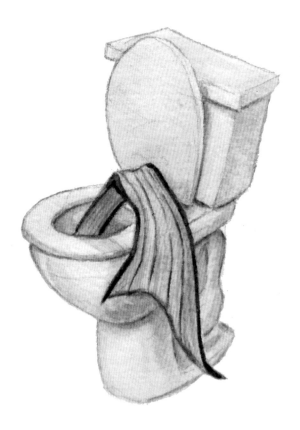

Then on Wednesday Billy's
mother found clothes strewn
everywhere. She made him spend
hours cleaning up the mess.
Again, Billy told her, "It wasn't
me, Mom! It was a monster!"

A lurching Laundry Monster had leaped out of the laundry basket! Billy was able to swat and slash the cloth creature until it was only a pile of dirty underwear and grungy socks on the floor.

The worst was on Thursday when Billy's mother found stinky garbage littered all over the kitchen floor. "But it wasn't me, Mom! It was a monster!" Billy told her.

The kitchen mess had been made by a revolting Bulbous Blob Monster. It had eaten everything in the kitchen! Billy had climbed on top of its monstrous belly and jumped until finally . . .

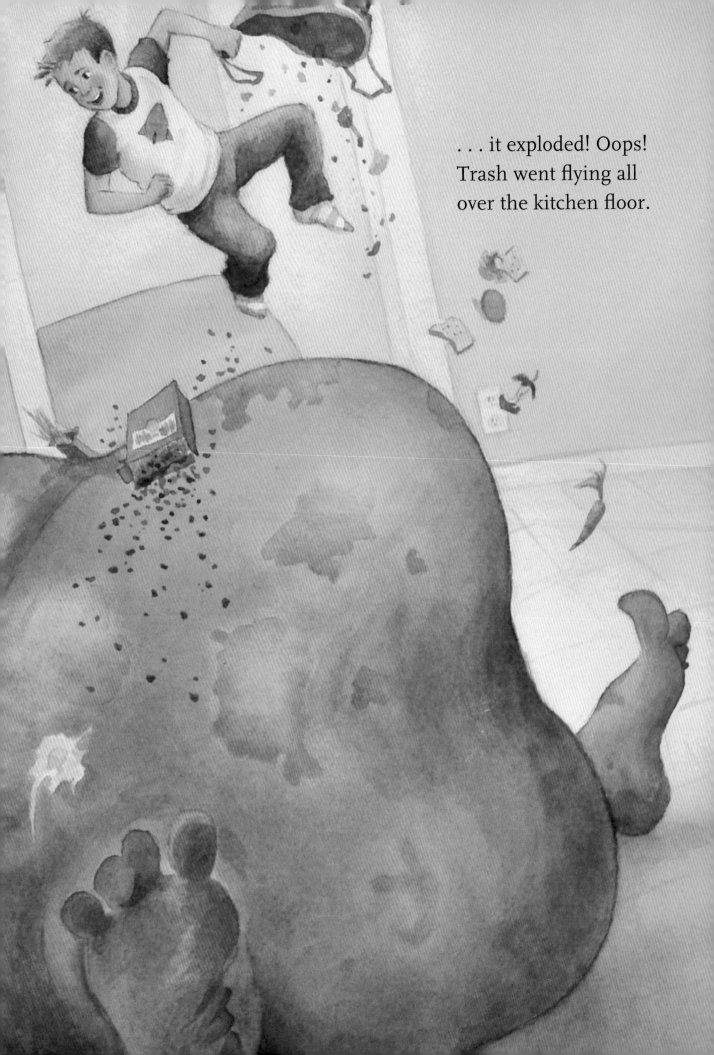

. . . it exploded! Oops! Trash went flying all over the kitchen floor.

Finally, on Friday, Billy's mother had had enough of his monster messes. She took all his toys and monster-fighting weapons away. "Until you start cleaning up after yourself, these are the only toys you'll be playing with," she said, as she handed Billy a vacuum and a bucket of warm, soapy water.

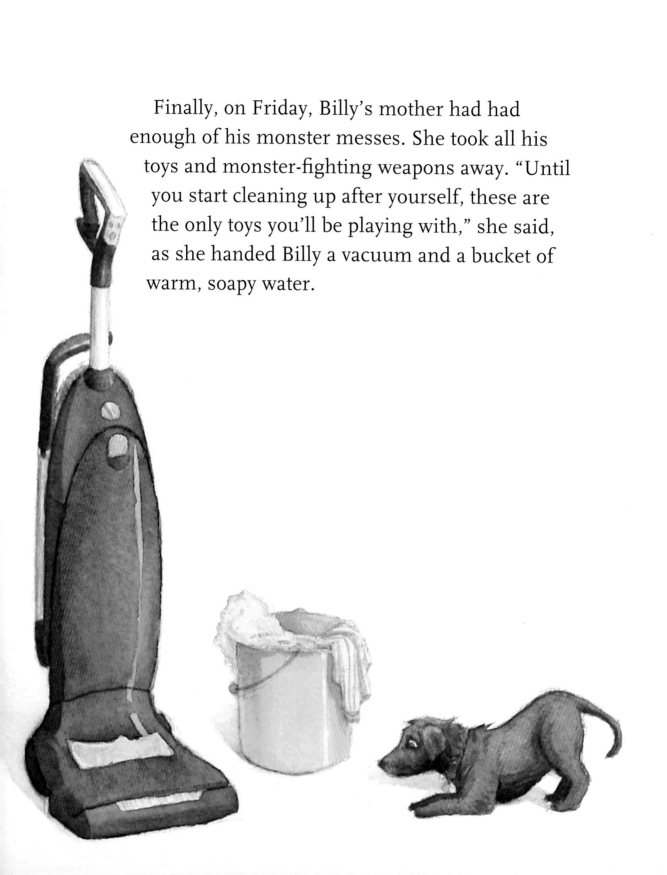

Billy was very upset. If only there was a way he could fight monsters and not make a mess.

Just then a giant Gloppy Grass Clod Monster shuffled into the kitchen. Billy was trapped! Then suddenly a thought came to him.

Billy quickly switched on the
vacuum and leapt forward with a
fearsome roar!

In no time he vacuumed, cleaned, and scrubbed up the grimy monster until it was nothing but a helpless lump of muck and mud in the vacuum bag. It had been the fastest monster cleanup ever!

Now Billy has a way to get rid of monsters and keep his house clean.

Varoooooooooom!
Bye-bye monsters!

Billy's mother was so happy that on Saturday she helped him make the best costume ever. He was now a real-life Monster Hunter! From that time on, whenever Billy had to clean up a mess, he had a special Monster Hunter suit to wear . . .

. . . because at Billy's house, you can be sure another monster is just waiting to come out and make a mess.

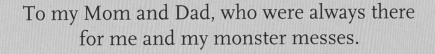

To my Mom and Dad, who were always there
for me and my monster messes.

Copyright © 2012 by Justin LaRocca Hansen

All Rights Reserved. No part of this book may be reproduced in any manner without the express
written consent of the publisher, except in the case of brief excerpts in critical reviews or articles.
All inquiries should be addressed to Sky Pony Press,
307 West 36th Street, 11th Floor, New York, NY 10018.

Sky Pony Press books may be purchased in bulk at special discounts for sales promotion,
corporate gifts, fund-raising, or educational purposes. Special editions can also be created to
specifications. For details, contact the Special Sales Department, Sky Pony Press,
307 West 36th Street, 11th Floor, New York, NY 10018 or info@skyhorsepublishing.com.

Sky Pony® is a registered trademark of Skyhorse Publishing, Inc.®, a Delaware corporation.

Visit our website at www.skyponypress.com.

10 9 8 7 6 5 4 3 2 1

Manufactured in China, June 2012
This product conforms to CPSIA 2008

Library of Congress Cataloging-in-Publication Data

Hansen, Justin LaRocca.
Monster hunter / Justin LaRocca Hansen.
p. cm.
Summary: At his mother's insistence, Billy finds a way to fight monsters without making a mess.
ISBN 978-1-61608-968-9 (hardcover : alk. paper)
[1. Monsters--Fiction. 2. Cleanliness--Fiction. 3. Imagination--Fiction.] I. Title.
PZ7.H19825iMo 2012
[E]--dc23
2012015602